GREEDYGUTS

Martina Selway

HUTCHINSON

London Sydney Auckland Johannesburg

Long, long ago, there was a young boy called Jack,
who lived with his family and friends in a village
called Wigwig. It was a beautiful village, right in
the heart of the countryside, and Jack thought it the
most perfect place in the world – except for one
thing . . .

GREEDYGUTS – the terror of their lives.

Now, Greedyguts was small for a giant, only about as tall as a house, but he was incredibly FAT and MEAN. He never stopped eating from morning to night, and when he ran out of food his tummy rumbles would roll across the countryside like thunder.

The rumbles were followed by the *stomp, stomp, stomp* of giant footsteps as Greedyguts strode over to Wigwig to grab anything he wanted. It took him so little time to reach the village, that the people had to scurry home quickly to lock their windows and bolt their doors.

The whole village, from the smallest child to the wisest old woman, hated and feared the giant, but what could they do? They were far too small and weak to frighten him. Even big Frederick the blacksmith, who was so strong he could bend an iron bar with his bare hands, was not big enough to scare Greedyguts.

It was at harvest time that Greedyguts was at his greediest. He would bring his big cart and help himself to the stores in the great barn. He would take wheat, barley, oats, potatoes and anything else he fancied.

The giant always took the best of everything.
'There's nothing that can be done,' sighed the
villagers as they gathered up what was left. This
infuriated Jack. He was determined that Greedyguts
should be stopped, but how?

One day, Jack was in his special thinking place,
dreaming of ways to trap the fat giant, when he
looked across the field and saw a colourful line of
people coming towards the village. There were
horses and carts, caravans, dogs and clowns – a fair
was visiting Wigwig!

Soon the whole village was buzzing with excitement. Even Jack forgot about the giant, until he looked up at the acrobats towering above him. 'They're even taller than Greedyguts,' he thought. Suddenly, he had a brilliant idea. If all the villagers got TOGETHER, maybe they could get rid of the big bully, once and for all!

That night, the people of Wigwig told the gypsies
about their BIG problem, and Jack explained how
the acrobats could help. After listening to his idea,
the gypsies agreed to teach the young people of the
village some of the tricks of their trade.

It wasn't easy! The gypsies worked hard to pass on
their skills, and they did not leave Wigwig until they
were sure that Jack's plan would work. All summer
long, the youngsters practised from dawn to dusk,
learning to work together.

Soon the harvest was gathered in and it was time to
celebrate. But the villagers knew that Greedyguts
would be getting hungry again and, sure enough, in
the middle of their harvest supper, they heard a
distant rumble followed by the *thud, thud, thud* of
giant footsteps.

'Let's go!' shouted Jack.

This was the moment they had been waiting for.
The young people climbed high on top of each other,
as they had been taught, while the rest of the
villagers gathered tools, pots and pans, and
anything that would make a loud noise.

Jack was just getting into position when the giant
came striding across the fields.

When Greedyguts was near, they all roared together
like a football crowd:

'GO AWAY GREEDYGUTS
AND NEVER COME HERE AGAIN.'

The giant stopped in his tracks. He had never
seen anyone bigger than himself before, nor so loud
and fearsome. He began to tremble. Greedyguts was
frightened!

Greedyguts turned on his heels and RAN.

He kept on running until he was only a dot on the landscape. He never once looked back – which was fortunate, because Jack was laughing so much that they all wobbled, lost their balance, and fell into a big heap.

From that day on, the village was never troubled by Greedyguts again, and the people of Wigwig lived happily ever after.

To John Aston

All rights reserved
First published in 1990 by Hutchinson Children's Books
an imprint of the Random Century Group Ltd
20 Vauxhall Bridge Road, London SW1V 2SA

Random Century Australia Pty Ltd
20 Alfred Street, Sydney, NSW 2061

Random Century New Zealand Ltd
PO Box 40-086, Glenfield, Auckland 10, New Zealand

Random Century South Africa (Pty) Ltd
PO Box 337, Bergvlei, 2012, South Africa

Designed by Paul Welti
Printed and bound in Belgium
by Proost International Book Production

British Library Cataloguing in Publication Data
Selway, Martina
Greedyguts.
I. Title
823'.914 [J]

ISBN 0 09 174151 3